ABIGAIL AND HER PET ZOMBIE

In this Life I would like to remind you;

That not every goal may come true,

That not all heroes may shine through,

That parents are not perfect,

And teachers always try their best, too.

That hope is the brightest light,

That dreams can take you to the greatest of heights,

That every victory no matter how big or small,

Is the path to the greatest discovery, you.

Marie F Crow

ABIGAIL AND HER PET ZOMBIE

Abigail doesn't have a pet fish.

Abigail doesn't have a pet hamster.

Abigail doesn't have a pet dog, or cat, or bird.

Abigail has a pet zombie.

Abigail's pet doesn't bark, or purr, or chirp.

Abigail's pet says ...... RAAAAAAAA

Abigail couldn't always play with her pet zombie.

Sometimes, she has to go to school.

It loves Abigail so much that sometimes her pet zombie becomes lonely.

It became so lonely, that one day
Abigail's pet zombie followed her to school.

Abigail's classmates were nervous at first, but soon they were laughing and playing with her pet zombie.

The teacher was not amused.

Abigail's pet zombie waited patiently
for the children to come outside to play.

WHEN it was finally time for recess, Abigail's pet zombie laughed and played with the children.

THEY SLID DOWN THE SLIDES.

It pushed them on the swings.

They played hide and seek.

Everyone was sad when the bell rang for recess to end.
The children didn't want to say goodbye to Abigail's pet zombie.

WHEN THE TEACHER SAW HOW GENTLE AND KIND Abigail's pet zombie was with the children, she invited it inside to join them for the day.

The children enjoyed having Abigail's pet zombie in class.

It was the best at art.

It was a little slow in math, but at the end of the day,
it received a gold star for being the quietest in the class.

Abigail's pet zombie doesn't follow her to school anymore.

Now, it waits at home.

It lingers and lingers and it waits and waits
for her and her classmates to come play.

When the school day ends, the children come to play.

They swing on the swings. They slide on the slide.

They play hide and seek and all the children say

that Abigail has the best pet of all. Abigail has a pet zombie.

More adventures from Abigail and her pet zombie coming soon.

www.mariefcrow.com

Email: info@mariefcrow.com

Follow Marie F Crow on Twitter:

https://twitter.com/MarieFCrow

Like Marie F Crow on Facebook:

www.facebook.com/MarieFCrow.Author

CPSIA information can be obtained
at www.ICGtesting.com
Printed in the USA
LVHW070226091218
599804LV00001B/2/P